Strawberry Shortcake Characters and Designs © 1983 American Greetings Corporation. TM* designates trademarks of American Greetings Corporation.

Library of Congress Cataloging in Publication Data: Doyle, Elizabeth. Strawberry Shortcake and the birthday surprise. SUMMARY: Raspberry Tart is convinced that all her friends have forgotten her birthday when she tries in vain to find someone to play with.
[1.   Birthdays—Fiction]   I.   Sustendal, Pat, ill.
II.   Title.   PZ7.D774St   1983   [E]   83-8168   ISBN 0-910313-11-3
Manufactured in the United States of America   2 3 4 5 6 7 8 9 0

Strawberry Shortcake

and the Birthday Surprise

Story by Elizabeth Doyle
Pictures by Pat Sustendal

Raspberry Tart couldn't fall asleep. Tomorrow was her birthday—a day that might be the best of the whole year.

Raspberry Tart thought about last year. What fun it had been to plan her party with the rest of the Kids. And the presents! There had even been a special treat, a new bicycle.

But this year nobody had mentioned a party, and it looked like no one would remember her birthday. She felt sad. What if everyone in Strawberryland, including Strawberry Shortcake, had forgotten that tomorrow was Raspberry's special day?

Raspberry Tart tossed and turned, but she finally fell asleep. Raspberry dreamed a wonderful dream about a big birthday party. All her friends were there—Blueberry Muffin, Orange Blossom, Angel Cake, Lemon Meringue, and, of course, Strawberry Shortcake.

They had all come to her party, and they had even brought their pets. Everyone gave her a present, and streamers and laughter swirled everywhere.

But in the morning when Raspberry Tart woke up, her house was very quiet. Raspberry hummed a special cheer-up song she knew, but nobody came to wish her a happy birthday.

"Well," Raspberry finally said out loud. "If no one will come to visit me, I will just have to go to visit them."

Raspberry Tart dialed Blueberry Muffin's number.

"Hello, Blueberry," she said, "Can I play with you and Cheesecake today?"

"I can't play today," answered Blueberry Muffin. "I have pies to bake."

Raspberry Tart next called Orange Blossom. "Hello, Orange Blossom," she said, "Could you meet me at the park today?"

Orange Blossom answered, "I'd like to, but I can't. I have to finish painting an important picture by three o'clock. If I go out to play, my painting won't get done."

"Oh, all right then," Raspberry answered in a sharp voice. "I'm sure that I can find someone who isn't so *very busy* to play with me." And she quickly hung up.

Raspberry Tart knew that sometimes you have better luck just going to a friend's house instead of phoning first. So she put on her hat and walked out the front door. Rhubarb went with her.

They walked down the road until they came to Angel Cake's house. Raspberry Tart knocked, and Angel Cake came to the door.

"Would you like to come to the park with us?" Raspberry asked.

"Oh thank you very much, but I just can't today."

Raspberry Tart was very disappointed. "Who cares about that little Angel Cake anyway," she thought. "I'll find someone better to play with."

With Rhubarb at her side, Raspberry went straight to Lemon Meringue's house. She called to her from the front walk.

"Would you like to play with us in the park?"

"I would like to, but I must wash my hair, so that it will look pretty at the special party I am going to. Maybe I can play tomorrow."

"It isn't fair," Raspberry said to Rhubarb. "Why should Lemon get to go to a party when it's *my* birthday? I'm the one who should be going to a party. Oh, why didn't anyone remember?"

She thought she would try one more place, but when she got to Huckleberry Pie's house, there was a big sign on the door: GONE FISHING WITH STRAWBERRY SHORTCAKE.

Raspberry Tart sat down on Huckleberry Pie's front porch and began to cry. As she cried, she thought to herself, "I will always remember how everybody forgot my birthday! They will be sorry that they were so mean to me!"

Raspberry Tart turned to Rhubarb Monkey and spoke in a firm voice: "You and I—we're going to have our own party in the park! We'll make a mud pie and seed cake. We will not invite the other Kids, but we will ask some birds to share it with us. The birds can sing Happy Birthday, then we can climb some trees and look at their babies."

Rhubarb smiled and clapped his hands, and off they went.

Raspberry Tart and Rhubarb Monkey had their party with the birds.

Then they went to find a good tree to climb.

Rhubarb Monkey climbed quickly and easily. When he spotted a pretty nest with two baby birds in it, he motioned to Raspberry Tart, "There are babies in this nest. Come and see them."

Raspberry Tart started up the tree, but she did not get very far. When she was only a few feet from the ground, she lost her footing and fell with a thump.

Although she was not hurt, Raspberry wanted to leave the park. She had had enough tree climbing. Everything seemed to be going wrong today.

As Raspberry and Rhubarb walked home, they passed a store. "Rhubarb," announced Raspberry Tart, "I know that nobody else is going to give me a present, so I will give myself one. It will cheer me up."

Raspberry Tart looked at pretty necklaces and pins. Finally she chose a seashell bracelet.

All the way home, Raspberry Tart looked at her beautiful new bracelet. She was pleased with it. It did make her feel a little better.

"This has been a long, long day," said Raspberry as they came to her house. "I think that I will go to my room and take a little nap."

As she walked up to her front door, it opened slowly.
There stood Strawberry Shortcake with a big smile and a
bunch of flowers.

"HAPPY BIRTHDAY," she sang.

When Raspberry Tart walked inside, there was an even bigger surprise. All her friends were in the living room—and in the corner was a heap of presents!

"What a lucky girl I am," thought Raspberry Tart. "I thought that everyone had forgotten me, but now I see that they were really trying to surprise me. Friends don't usually forget each other's special days."

Strawberry Shortcake took charge. She called
everyone to the table. It was time for the birthday cake.

After everyone sang Happy Birthday, Raspberry Tart blew out the candles.

Raspberry Tart opened all her presents.

Then the the Kids all hunted for peanuts. They pinned
the tail on the donkey.

They had a balloon-blowing contest.

Finally Strawberry Shortcake said, "I have a poem for you. Here it is."

A day that's special
Just for you!
Your birthday is here
            And we are too!
Together we sing,
Together we play,
Together we celebrate
            Your special day!

When the party was over, Raspberry Tart stood at the door and waved goodbye to most of her friends.

The day was almost over, but there was one more
special treat. For Strawberry Shortcake had decided to sleep
over that night!

As she snuggled under her blankets, Raspberry Tart thought about her day. She smiled and felt like the happiest girl in Strawberryland.

Happy birthday, Raspberry Tart. And good night!